Copyright © 2008 by Jeff Mack

A Neal Porter Book
Published by Roaring Brook Press
Roaring Brook Press is a division of Holzbrinck Publishing Holdings Limited Partnership
175 Fifth Avenue, New York, New York 10010
All rights reserved
mackids.com

Library of Congress Cataloging-in-Publication Data

Mack, Jeff.
Hush little polar bear / Jeff Mack. — 1st ed.
p. cm.
Summary: A little girl invites her plush polar bear to dream of all the places
where sleeping bears go, from the high seas to a starry desert and back home.
ISBN 978-1-59643-368-7
[1. Stories in rhyme. 2. Bedtime—Fiction. 3. Dreams—Fiction. 4. Adventure and
adventures—Fiction. 5. Polar bear—Fiction. 6. Bears—Fiction.] I. Title.
PZ8.3.M1747Hus 2008
[E]—dc22
  2007044049

Roaring Brook Press books are available for special promotions and premiums.
For details, contact: Director of Special Markets, Holzbrinck Publishers.

Printed in China by RR Donnelley Asia Printing Solutions Ltd., Dongguan City, Guangdong Province.
First edition November 2008
10 9 8 7 6 5

Hush Little Polar Bear

JEFF MACK

 A NEAL PORTER BOOK   ROARING BROOK PRESS   NEW YORK

Hush little polar bear.
Sleep in the snow,
and dream of the places
where sleeping bears go.

Sail the high seas on the back of a whale.

Land on a beach,
and then follow a trail.

Wade through a marsh
where the tall grasses grow,

where butterflies flutter
and warm breezes blow.

Bounce through a pasture
where cows come to graze.

Creep through a cave
with an underground maze.

Swim through a waterfall.
Splash in a stream.
Paddle past rainbows
that glisten and gleam.

Swing through the trees from a dangling vine.

Forge through a desert where stars shimmer and shine.

Climb a tall mountain where
billy goats play,
where breezes grow cooler
and clouds fade away.

Leap from the peak

and then float through the sky.

Soar as the hawks and the eagles fly by.

Dive through the clouds
to a town far below
with the lights from the streetlamps
and houses aglow.

Drift through my window.
Crawl into bed.
Curl up beside me
and rest your sweet head.

Pretend that you're sleeping
and dreaming like me.

Then look right beside you,
and that's where I'll be.